Monsters

A Step-by-Step Guide for the Aspiring Monster-Maker

Tony Tallarico

Dover Publications, Inc.
Mineola, New York

Bibliographical Note

This Dover edition, first published in 2010, is an unabridged republication of the work originally published by The Putnam Publishing Group, New York, in 1992.

International Standard Book Number

ISBN-13: 978-0-486-47278-2
ISBN-10: 0-486-47278-7

Manufactured in the United States by RR Donnelley
47278702   2015
www.doverpublications.com

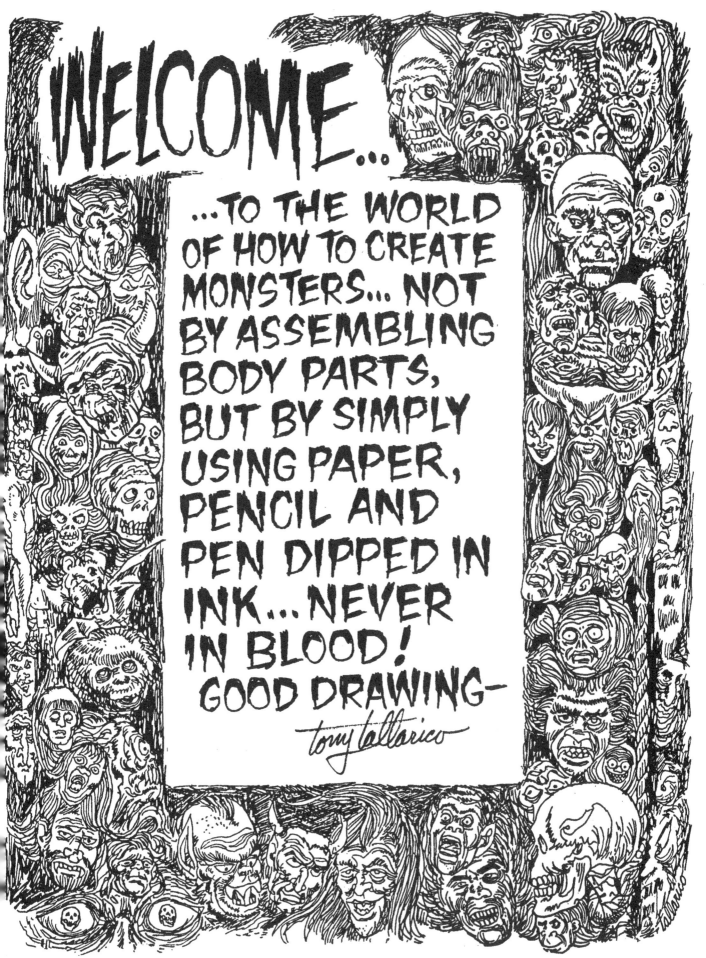

WELCOME...

...TO THE WORLD OF HOW TO CREATE MONSTERS... NOT BY ASSEMBLING BODY PARTS, BUT BY SIMPLY USING PAPER, PENCIL AND PEN DIPPED IN INK... NEVER IN BLOOD! GOOD DRAWING—

Tony Tallarico

COMPARATIVE PROPORTIONS

Monsters come in all sizes and shapes.
Here are what a few look like in comparison
to an average six-foot human male.

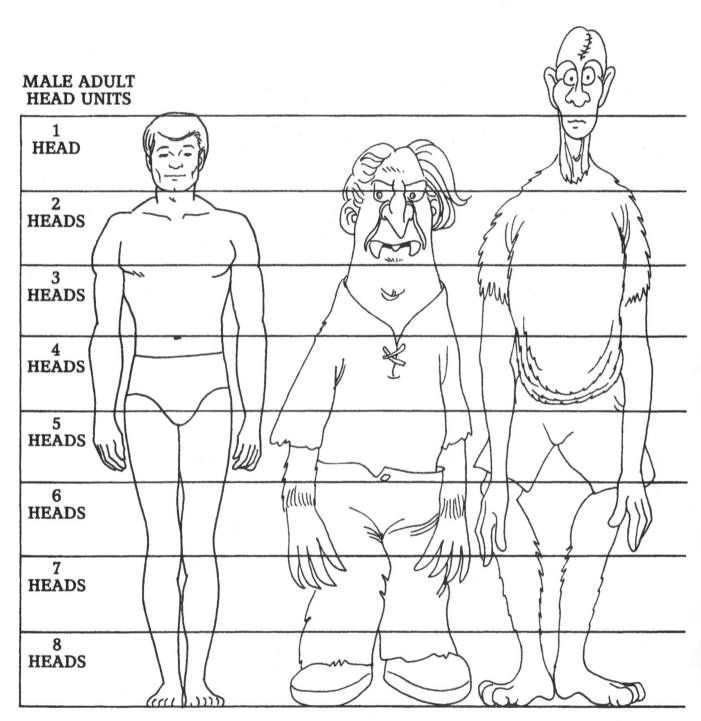

**MALE ADULT
HEAD UNITS**

1 HEAD	
2 HEADS	
3 HEADS	
4 HEADS	
5 HEADS	
6 HEADS	
7 HEADS	
8 HEADS	

Let's not forget that there are female
monsters too . . . and here is a comparison
chart for them.

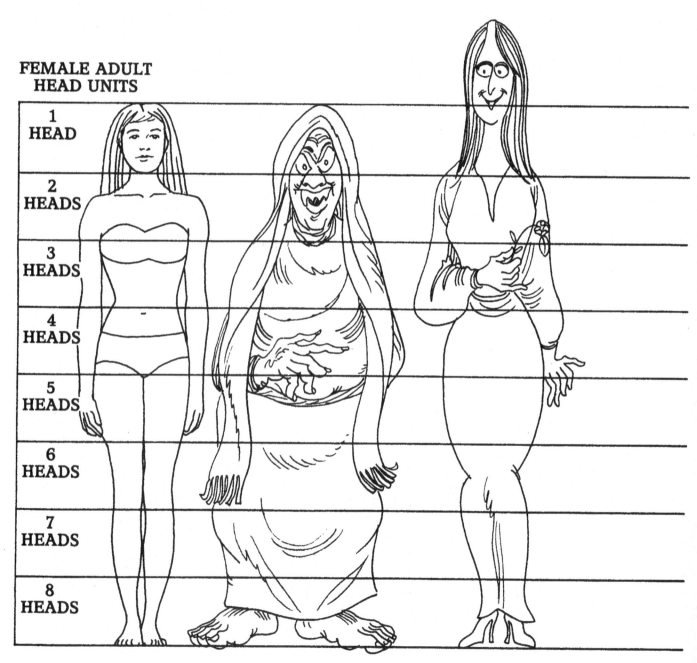

FEMALE ADULT
HEAD UNITS

1 HEAD	
2 HEADS	
3 HEADS	
4 HEADS	
5 HEADS	
6 HEADS	
7 HEADS	
8 HEADS	

Many little monsters are about eleven years
of age. How do they compare to a human of the
same size? See for yourself.

**11-YEAR-OLD BOY
HEAD UNITS**

1 HEAD	
2 HEADS	
3 HEADS	
4 HEADS	
5 HEADS	
6 HEADS	
7 HEADS	

Let's not leave out that sweet little six-year-old . . .
she's charming and polite and also a monster.

6-YEAR-OLD GIRL
HEAD UNITS

1 HEAD

2 HEADS

3 HEADS

4 HEADS

5 HEADS

6 HEADS

HOW TO BEGIN

On the past few pages you might have noticed a very important thing about drawing monsters . . . there are NO definite proportions.

The man, woman, boy and girl shown all are based on the eight-heads-high proportion. Since all monsters are imaginary—no proportion exists. In a way, this makes drawing monsters easier than drawing people, animals, etc., which are based on actual things. But the basic procedure is the same.

ALL drawing is based on basic shapes.

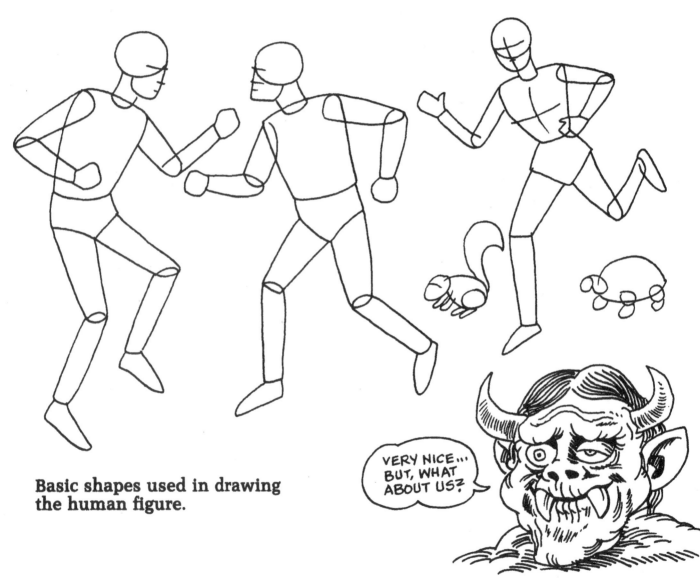

Basic shapes used in drawing the human figure.

VERY NICE.... BUT, WHAT ABOUT US?

1— ...mine and ... the basic

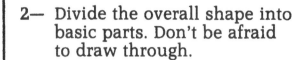

2— Divide the overall shape into basic parts. Don't be afraid to draw through.

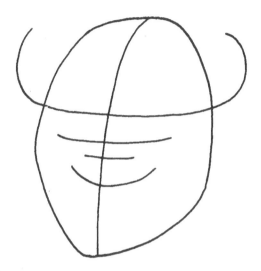

THE HEAD

3— Now start adding basic details— still, don't be afraid to draw through. Erasers have been invented and can be used.

4— Erase the guidelines and add all the details you want. You can't go wrong because everything is added to the basic shape.

I'm glad you're here. Now, if you'll hold still for a few minutes, I'll let our readers see exactly what is meant by drawing with basic shapes.

Always have an expression in mind when drawing a monster's face!

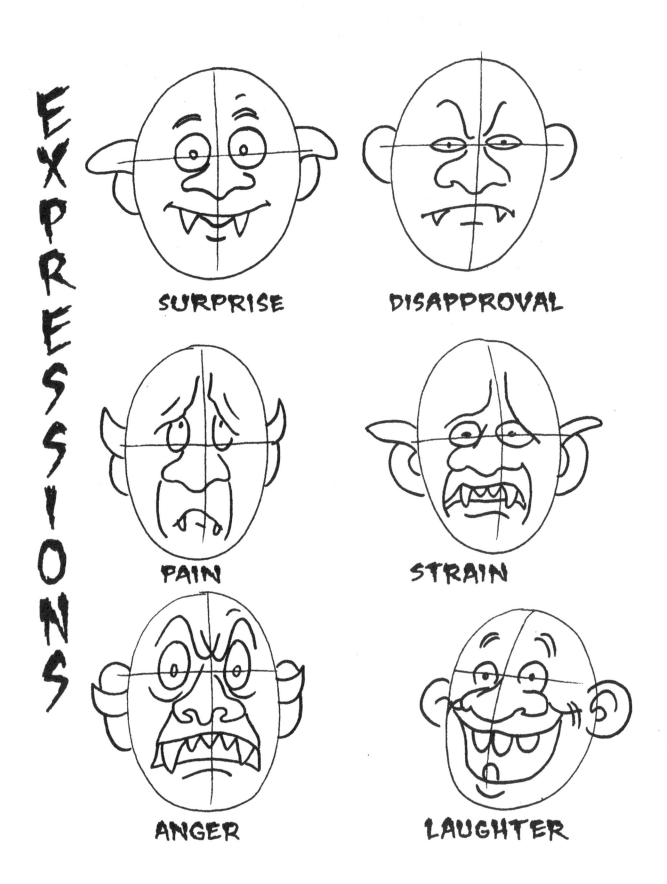

EXPRESSIONS

SURPRISE

DISAPPROVAL

PAIN

STRAIN

ANGER

LAUGHTER

At this stage, just use an oval shape and into this, draw the basic shapes of eyebrows, eyes and mouth to form these expressions.

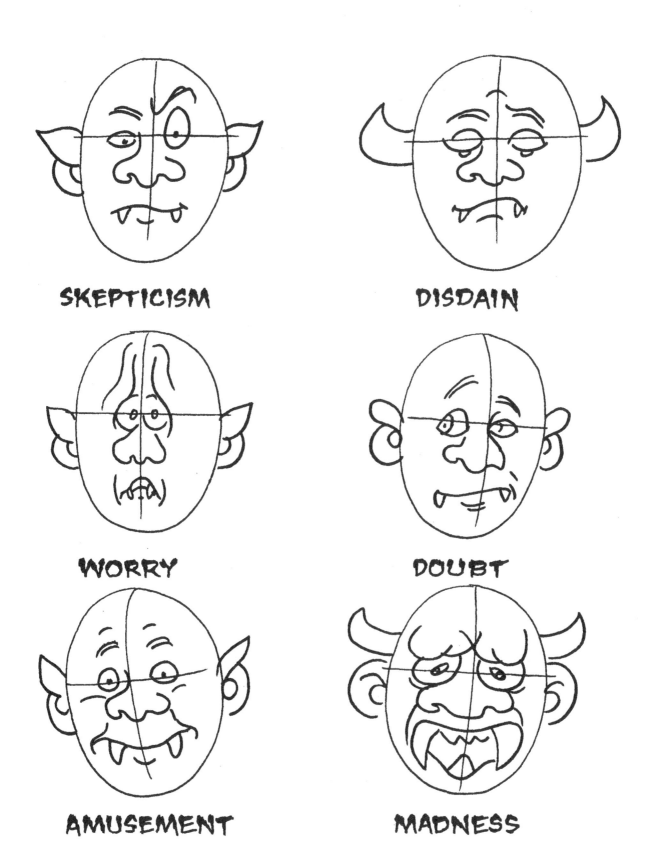

SKEPTICISM

DISDAIN

WORRY

DOUBT

AMUSEMENT

MADNESS

I'll now take you through the steps it takes to draw different monster faces. Notice that the basic shape is different in each case.

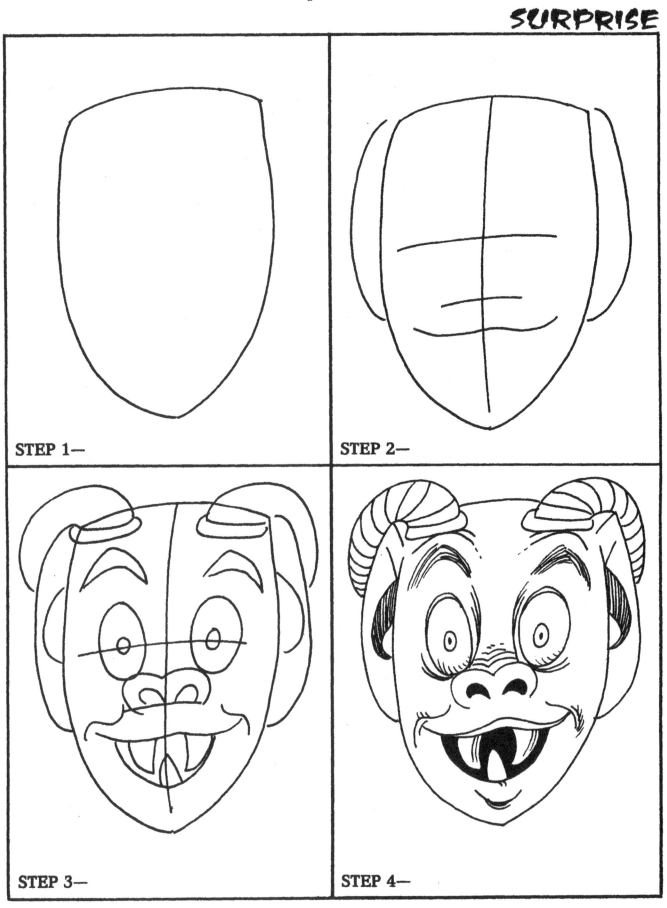

STEP 1—

STEP 2—

STEP 3—

STEP 4—

Always draw the first 3 steps lightly in pencil and don't be afraid to erase before going on to step number 4—the finished drawing.

DISAPPROVAL

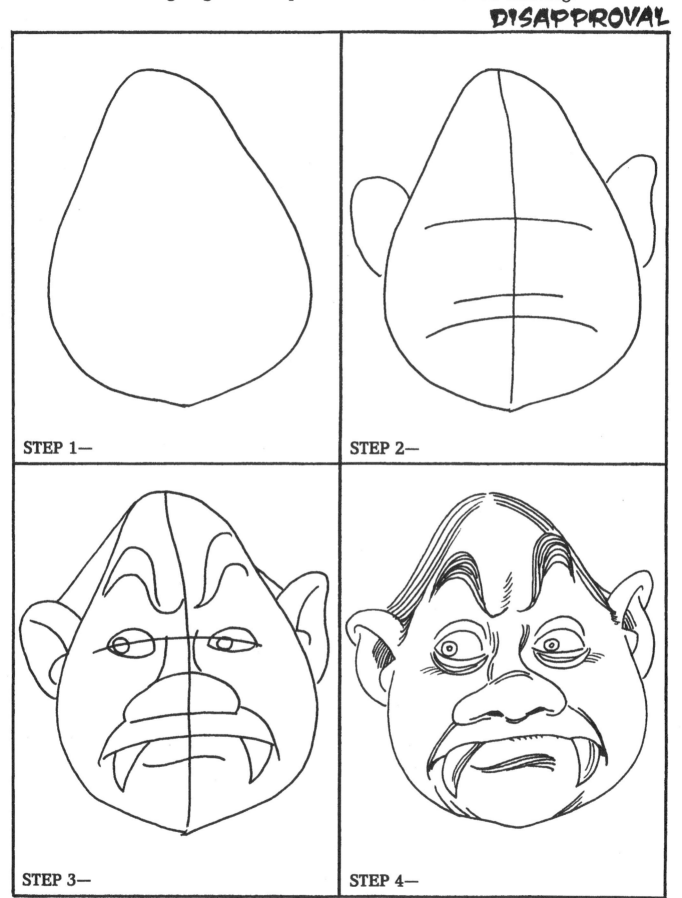

STEP 1—

STEP 2—

STEP 3—

STEP 4—

If you don't keep the first 3 steps drawn lightly in pencil, a monster is going to get you!

PAIN

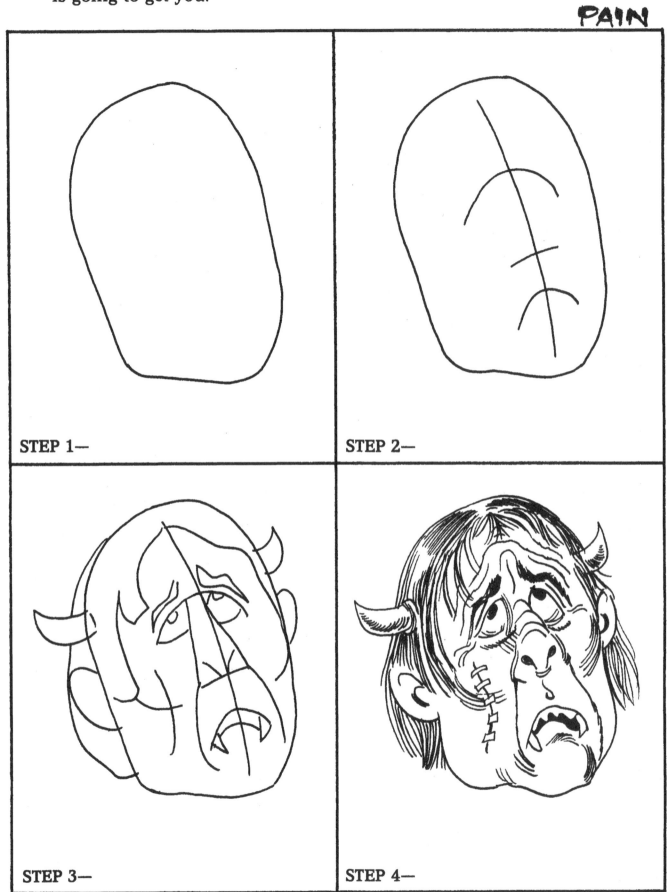

STEP 1—

STEP 2—

STEP 3—

STEP 4—

By drawing the first 3 steps lightly, you are in complete control and can easily change things.

STRAIN

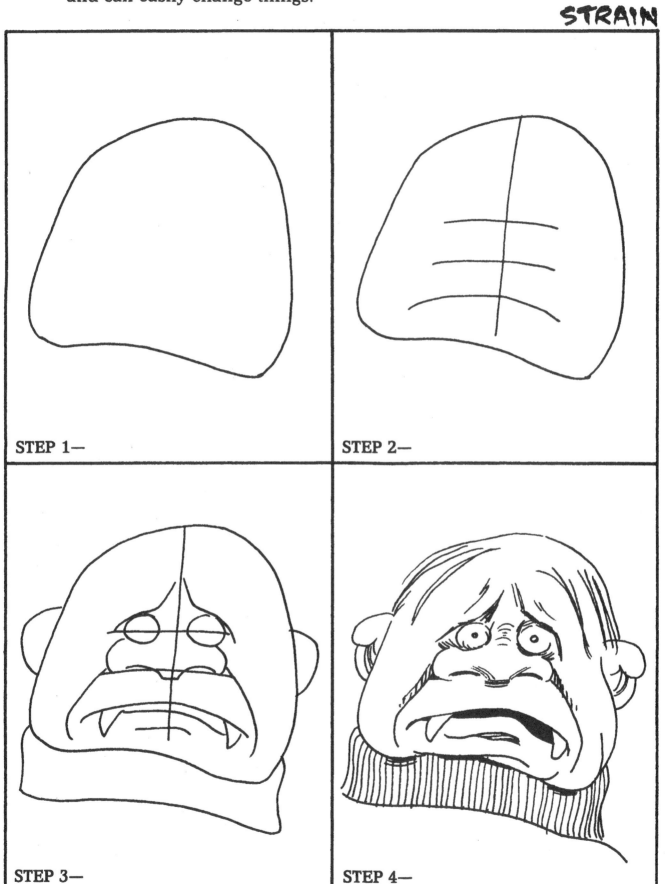

STEP 1—

STEP 2—

STEP 3—

STEP 4—

Never—I said never—try drawing the finished picture without going through steps 1, 2 and 3.

ANGER

STEP 1—

STEP 2—

STEP 3—

STEP 4—

All these expressions are exaggerations . . . but then, so are monsters.

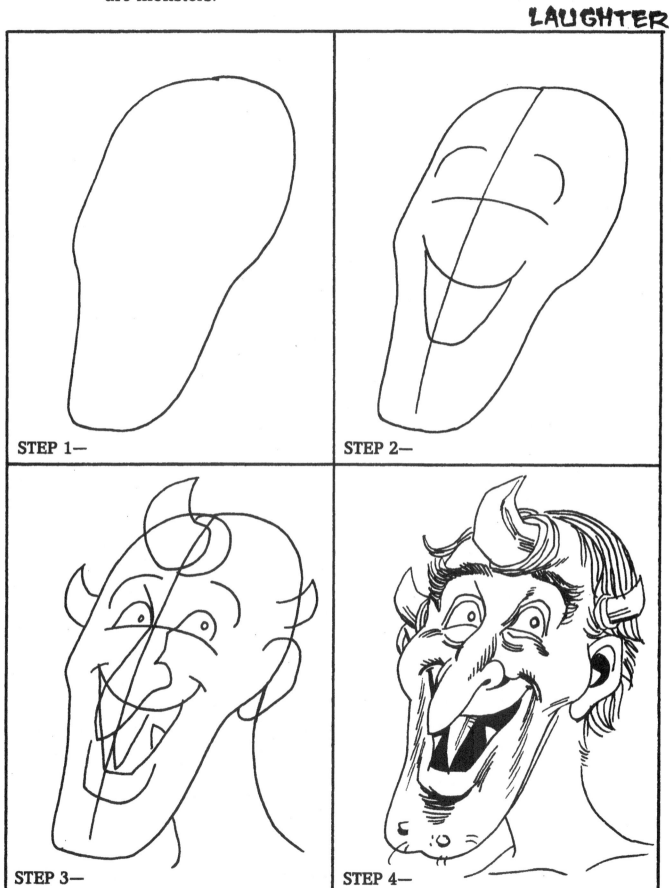

STEP 1—

STEP 2—

STEP 3—

STEP 4—

If you don't believe that basic steps are important, just draw this head with and without using them. Compare the two.

STEP 1—

STEP 2—

STEP 3—

STEP 4—

It may seem boring drawing the first 3 steps. But they are the basis of all good drawing.

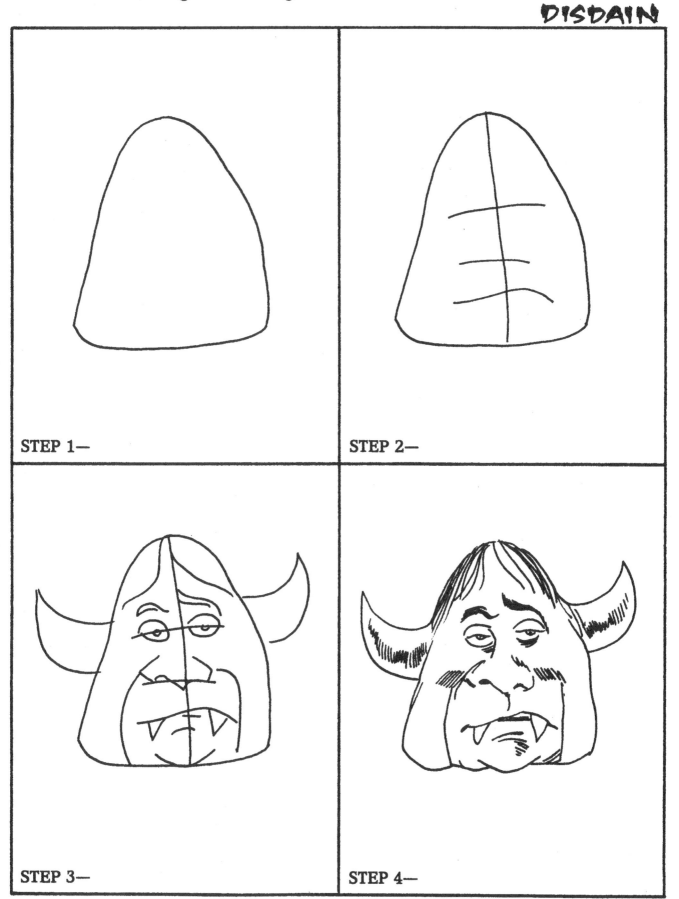

STEP 1—

STEP 2—

STEP 3—

STEP 4—

Basic steps are even more important when we start drawing
whole bodies . . .

WORRY

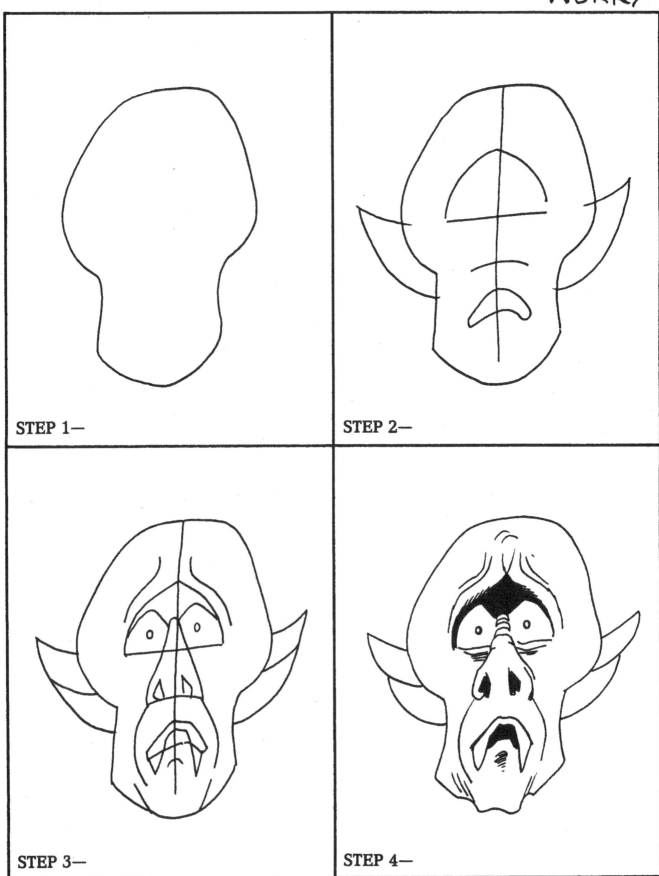

STEP 1—

STEP 2—

STEP 3—

STEP 4—

They become even more important when we start placing our monsters into situations.

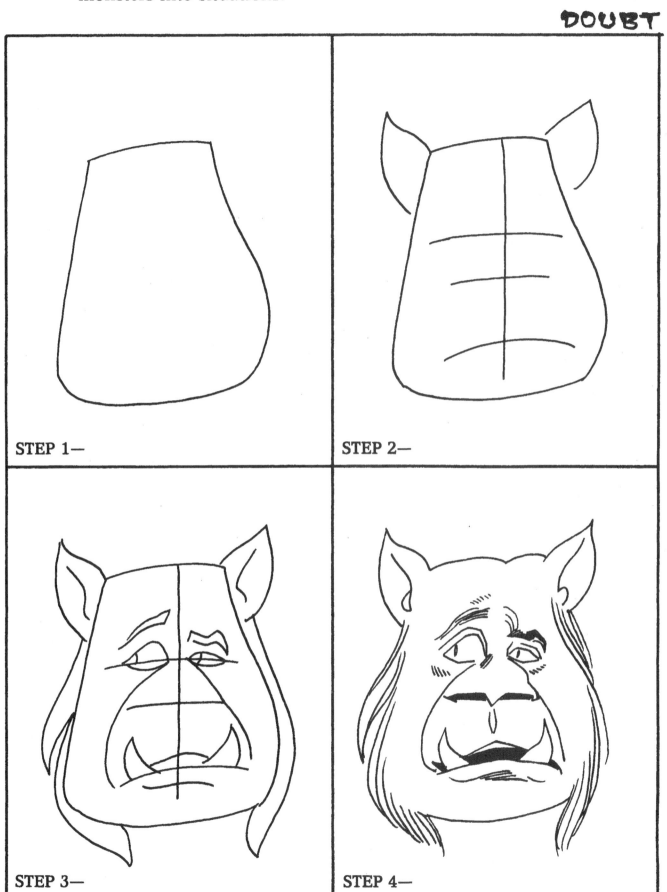

STEP 1—

STEP 2—

STEP 3—

STEP 4—

The basic shape will be destroyed in most instances by the addition of hair, etc., but never start without it.

STEP 1—

STEP 2—

STEP 3—

STEP 4—

On the next page are a few more expressions. Try drawing these using your own basic steps.

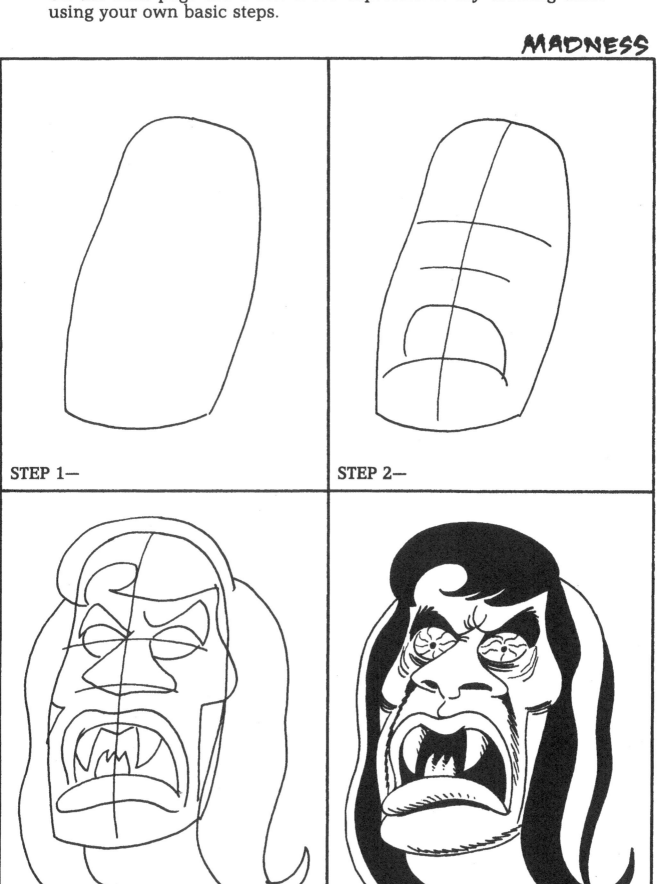

STEP 1—

STEP 2—

STEP 3—

STEP 4—

Draw these heads using your own basic shapes. Then add shading and details as shown on the next page.

DOUBT

SEDUCTIVE

ANGER

DISDAIN

SUPPLICATION

LAUGHTER

SKEPTICISM

FRIGHT

SURPRISE

DOUBT

SEDUCTIVE

ANGER

DISDAIN

SUPPLICATION

LAUGHTER

SKEPTICISM

FRIGHT

SURPRISE

LIGHTING THE HEAD —

The basic drawing.

1— Establish a light source.

2— Using a number 2 brush and black India ink—or a black marker —put shadows and blacks in.

3— Wherever light strikes the head— leave white. Be aware of cast shadows.

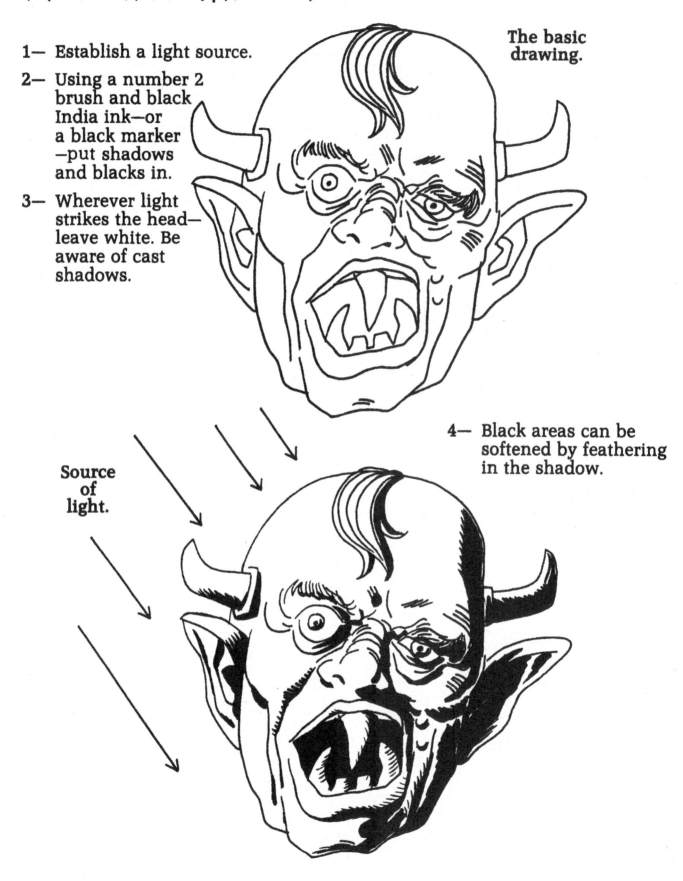

Source of light.

4— Black areas can be softened by feathering in the shadow.

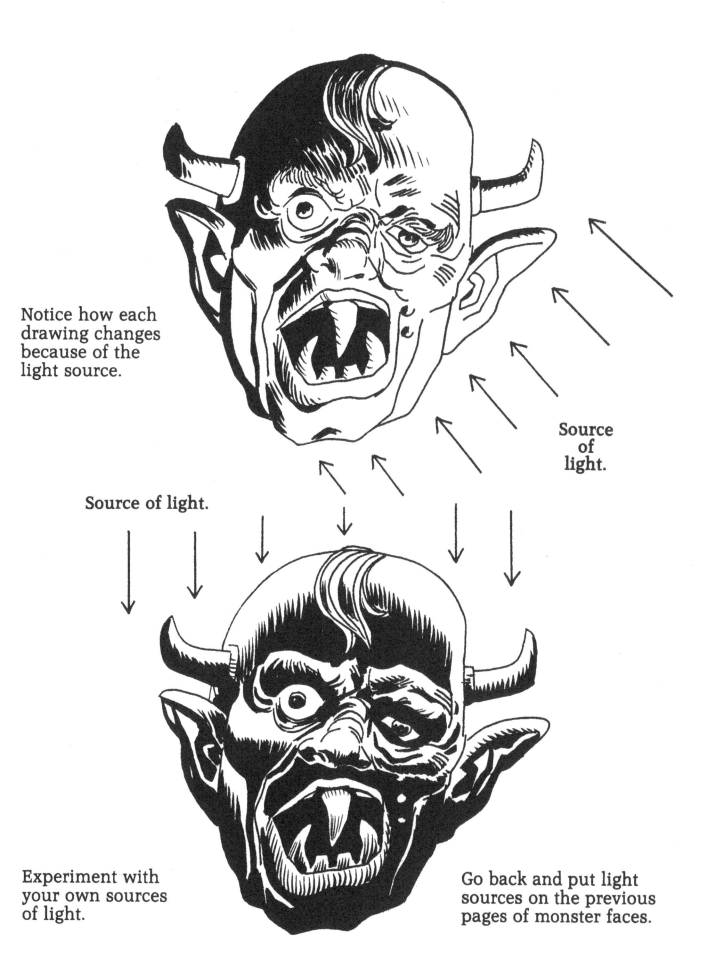

Notice how each drawing changes because of the light source.

Source of light.

Source of light.

Experiment with your own sources of light.

Go back and put light sources on the previous pages of monster faces.

THE WHOLE MONSTER

Just as in drawing the monster head, draw the basic shapes and keep adding to them.

Draw the hair dropping off from the basic shapes.

STEP 1—

STEP 2—

STEP 3—

STEP 4—

After you've completed your drawing, turn to the next page to learn how to add shadows to your monster figures.

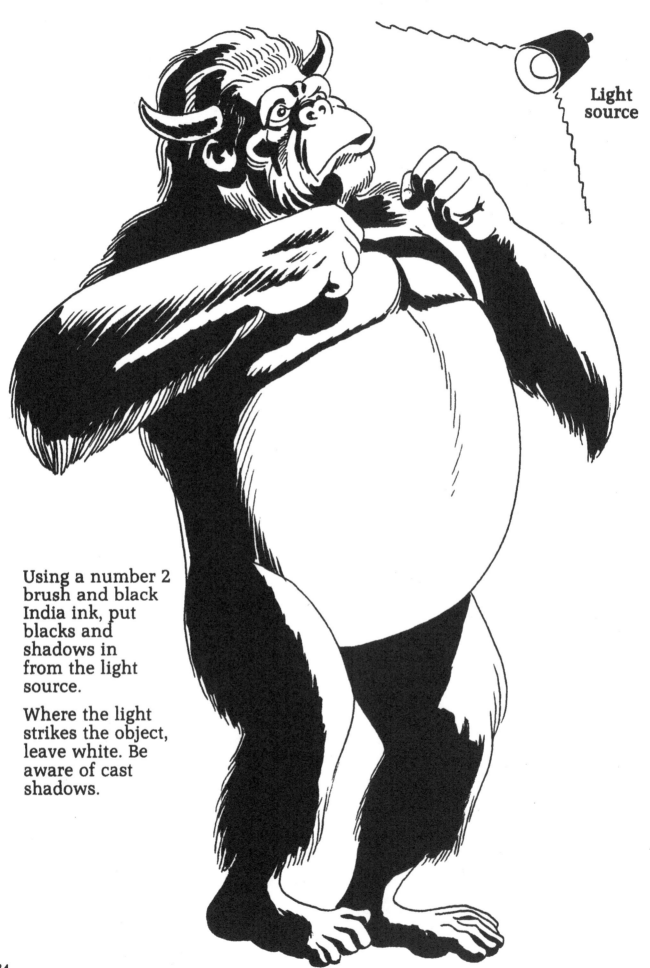

Light source

Using a number 2 brush and black India ink, put blacks and shadows in from the light source.

Where the light strikes the object, leave white. Be aware of cast shadows.

Vary your light sources and watch your drawing change. In drawing monsters, the more radical the light source, the better the picture.

All this started with the basic shapes.

Bottom light

Back light

This is a good exercise to learn the forms and shapes you have drawn.

WHAT'S A NICE-LOOKING GUY LIKE YOU DOING IN A BOOK LIKE THIS?

Establish a ground area so that your monster is not floating on the page.

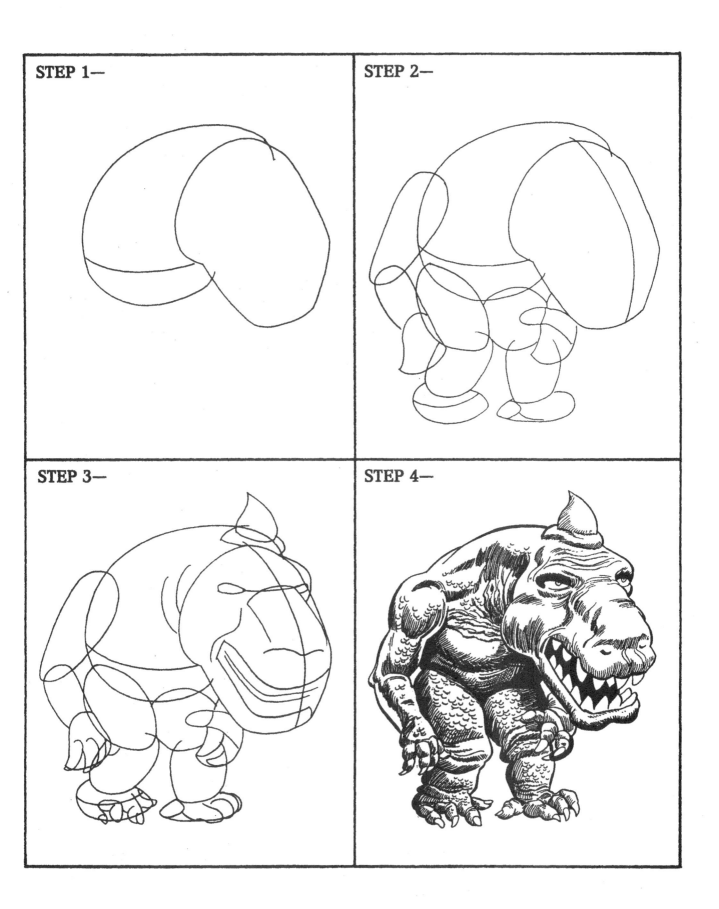

STEP 1—

STEP 2—

STEP 3—

STEP 4—

Do not try to add blacks and details until after you are satisfied with the basic shapes and proportions.

"WHAT'S FOR DINNER... YOU?"

A series of randomly placed short lines will indicate hair.

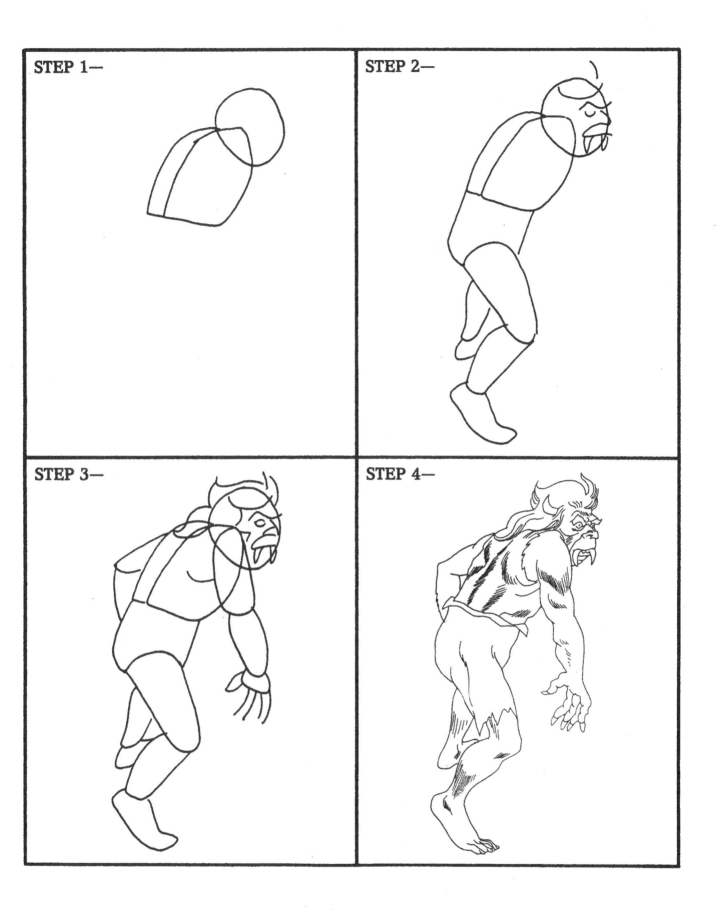

STEP 1—

STEP 2—

STEP 3—

STEP 4—

Try drawing this figure with the same basic shapes but with different proportions—such as a larger head or longer arms. However you change it, you must use the basic shapes to build on.

"I DON'T LIKE BROCCOLI!"

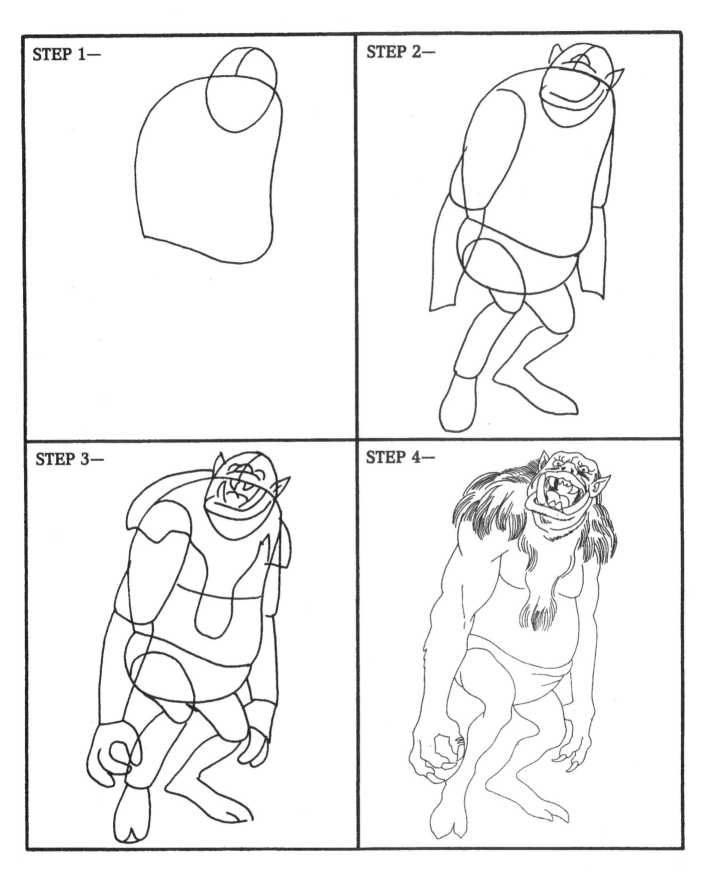

STEP 1—

STEP 2—

STEP 3—

STEP 4—

A few simple vertical lines give the illusion that this monster is standing in a pool of water . . . or blood.

"DID YOU HEAR THE ONE ABOUT THE TWO VAMPIRES THAT REACHED THEIR VICTIM AT EXACTLY THE SAME MOMENT? IT WAS A NECKTIE!"

Source of light.

Even in this light drawing of a monster, a source of light has been established.

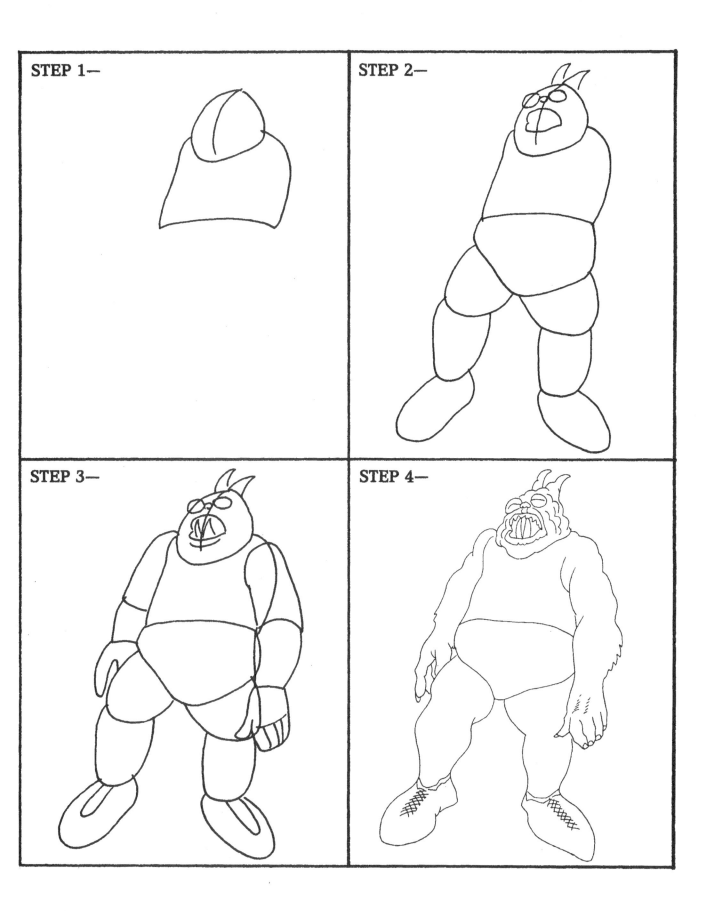

STEP 1—

STEP 2—

STEP 3—

STEP 4—

As simple as this monster may look to you, you still must build on the basic shapes before you add detail and lighting.

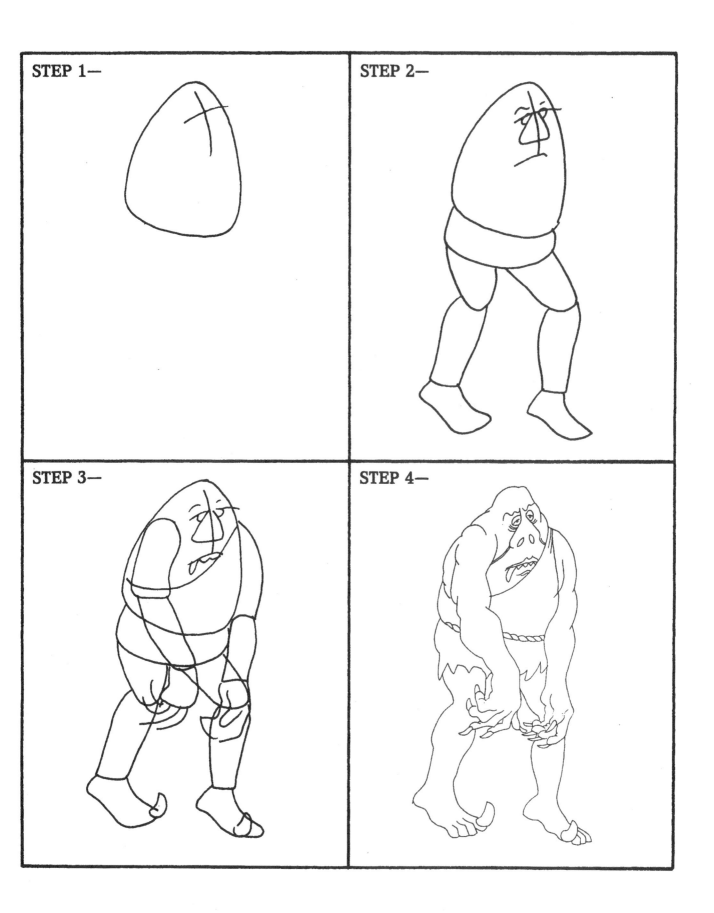

STEP 1—

STEP 2—

STEP 3—

STEP 4—

On this drawing there should be no doubt where the source of light is from.

"I CAN CURE HEADACHES!"

In what direction is the source of light coming from?

A series of short, parallel lines gives the illusion of a shiny metal or glass surface.

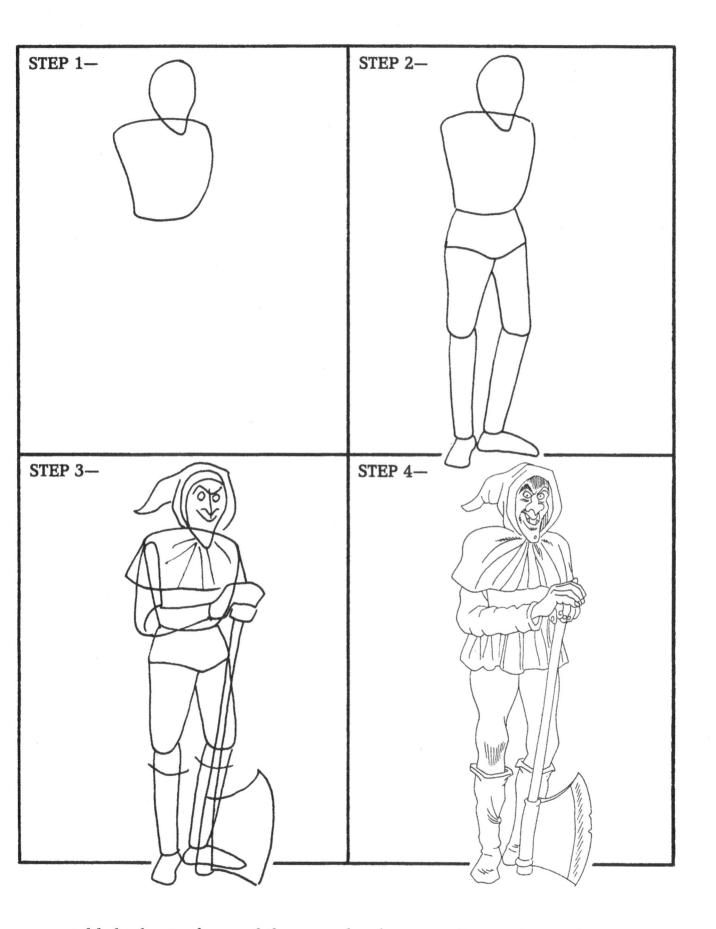

STEP 1—

STEP 2—

STEP 3—

STEP 4—

Add the basic shape of the ax only after your figure's basic shapes are complete.

STEP 1—

STEP 2—

STEP 3—

STEP 4—

Draw the basic shape for the boulder and water after the basic shapes for the figure have been put in.

MERLIN, MONSTER MAKER!

STEP 1—

STEP 2—

STEP 3—

STEP 4—

Draw all lines to one point on the skull to achieve this burst of energy effect.

"DO YOU NEED A HAIRCUT?"

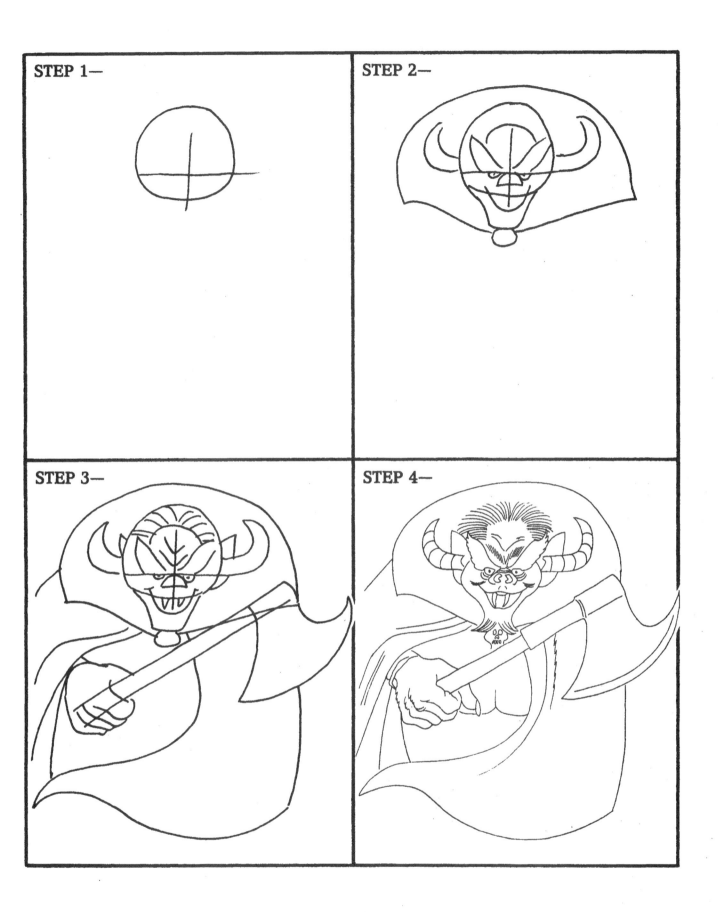

STEP 1—

STEP 2—

STEP 3—

STEP 4—

The black areas encircle the head, which is the focal point of the drawing.

IT'S BARBECUE TIME!

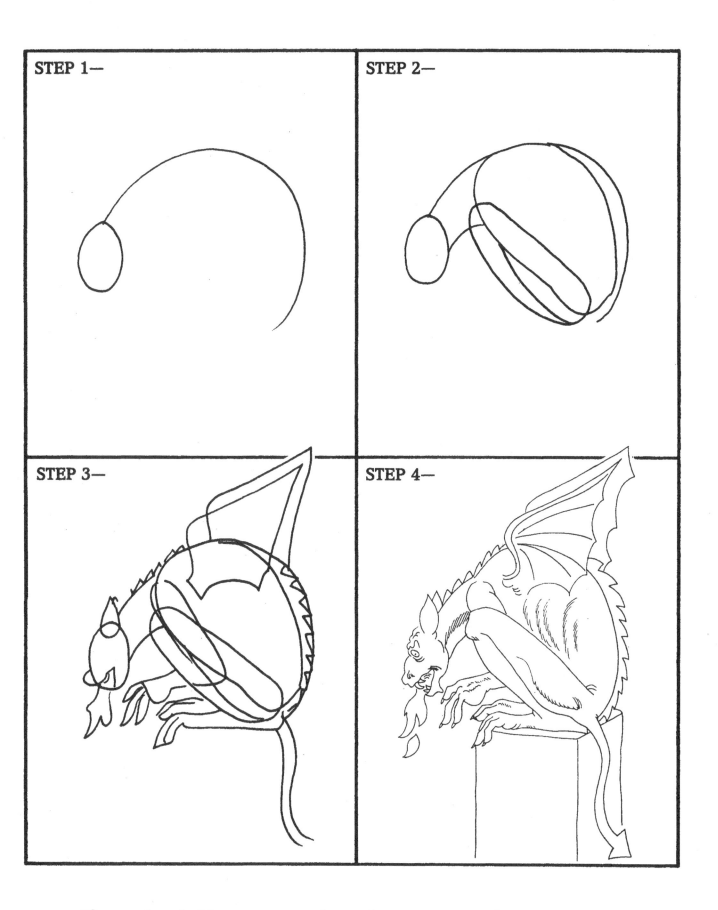

The roof and chimney are indicated so as not to take away from the focal point of the picture, which, of course, is the monster on your chimney.

GET THE MONSTER BUG SPRAY!!

Various cross-hatching used:

STEP 1—

STEP 2—

STEP 3—

STEP 4—

All the shadows in this drawing were put in by using pen and ink—
no solid blacks were used.

A KNIGHT OF THE MONSTER ROUND TABLE!

STEP 1—

STEP 2—

STEP 3—

STEP 4—

A combination of pen-and-ink technique and blacks was used in this drawing.

THIS IS NOT YOUR MUMMY!

Add action lines for movement.

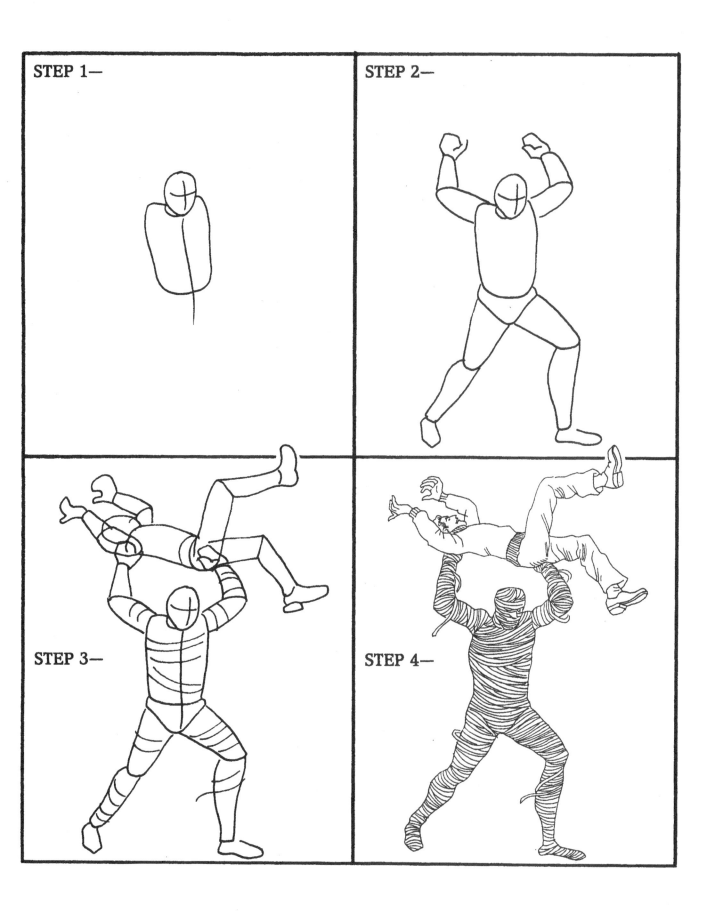

STEP 1—

STEP 2—

STEP 3—

STEP 4—

A simple pyramid and subtle ground cast shadows under the figures, adding depth to the action.

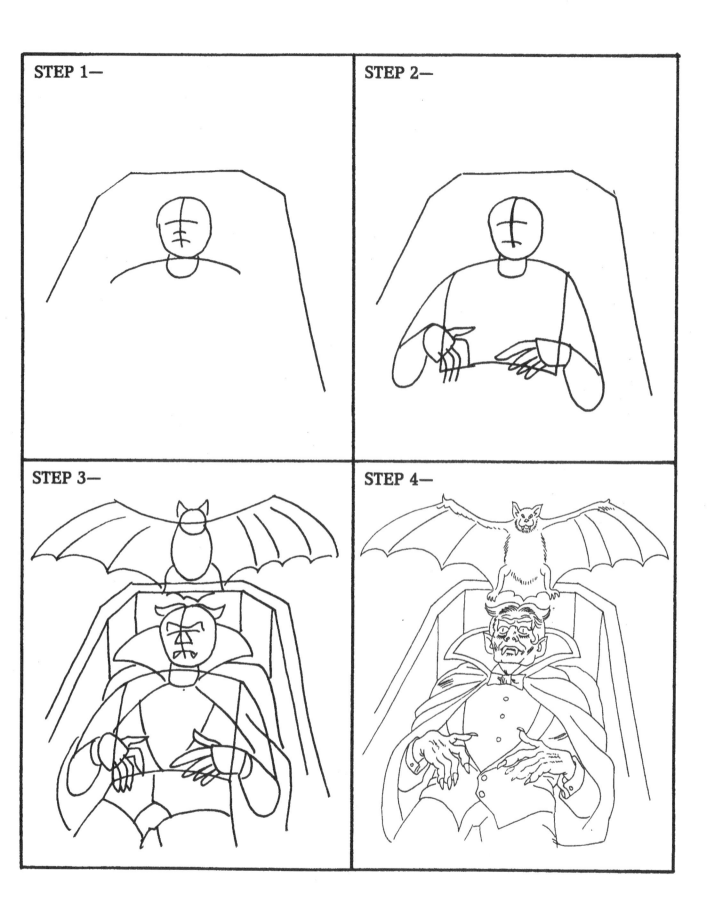

By adding a tone of texture to the picture, you succeed in tying the composition together.

SUMMONING THE UNDEAD!

STEP 1—

STEP 2—

STEP 3—

STEP 4—

An indication of a moon and the addition of a skull tombstone add to the overall feeling. The figure is backlit by the moon—but the tombstone is not.

COUNT DRACULA'S PROM DATE

STEP 1—

STEP 2—

STEP 3—

STEP 4—

The background is simple yet sets the stage and the mood of the picture. It does not interfere with the main subject matter.

YOU CAN BE HER
VALENTINE, TOO!

STEP 1—

STEP 2—

STEP 3—

STEP 4—

Blacks were used on the main figure only—the balance of the drawing was entirely done in pen and ink.

DRAWING MONSTER COMICS!

The following is an actual five-page comic book script—complete with rough layouts that interpret the script. The actual working layouts and finished art follow.

STEPS IN DOING BASIC COMIC STYLE LETTERING:
USING A B-6 LETTERING PEN OR FLAIR MARKER.

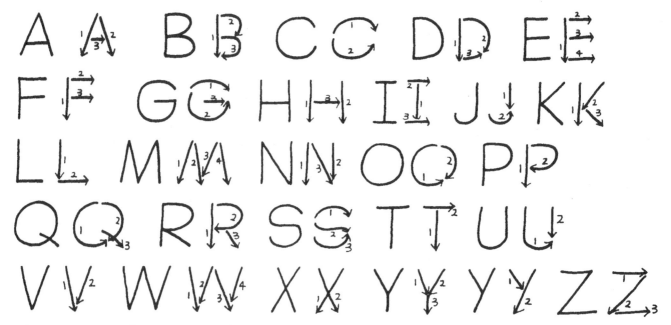

The same strokes are used in doing

MONSTER LETTERING!

The difference is, you are using a shaky line and building up the top area of each letter.

A B C D E F G H I-I
J K L M N O P Q
R S T U V W X Y Z

<u>STOP DAYDREAMING</u>

5-page comic book script

page 1

    panel 1: large dreamlike dragon/swordsman sequence with main
                 character (Harrison) looking muscular and dressed in
                 a loincloth, fighting a beast with sword.
                 "STOP DAYDREAMING" title over picture

    panel 2: college classroom scene; Harrison and other students
                 facing professor.

  Professor: "YOU'VE GOT YOUR DAYS AND NIGHTS MIXED UP AGAIN,
                 HARRISON!! PERHAPS YOU WOULD LIKE TO PAY THE DEAN
                 ANOTHER VISIT?"

   Harrison: (looking confused) "ULP!! HUH?"

panel 1: Harrison, Rita (holding books) and another male student outside classroom in hallway. Harrison stands between them looking tired and sad.

Rita: "YOU'RE GETTING TO BE MORE AND MORE LIKE A 'WALTER MITTY'!"

Male: "YOU'RE GONNA GET YOUR TAIL KICKED OUT OF HERE IF YOU DON'T KNOCK OFF THIS DAYDREAMING BIT!"

panel 2: Harrison and others making their way into another classroom.

Harrison: (thinking) "WALTER MITTY? HE DAYDREAMED OF WHAT HE WANTED TO BE ... MY THOUGHTS ARE OF WHAT I MUST DO!"

panel 3: Harrison and Rita sitting in class, facing teacher.

Harrison: (daydreaming) THE PROFESSOR'S VOICE FADED OUT OF PERSPECTIVE AS MY INNER THOUGHTS AGAIN RESUMED THE STRUGGLE ...

Teacher: "AGAIN AS YESTERDAY THE OBJECT OF THIS THEORY IS TO RECTIFY ... (words get smaller and fade out)

Harrison daydreams he's fighting a dragonlike monster.

Harrison: "WE MEET AGAIN!"

panel 4: Rita and Harrison in classroom - she nudges Harrison to wake him.

Rita: "HARRISON! FOR PETE'S SAKE - NOT IN THIS CLASS TOO! YOU'RE GOING TO BE SENT DOWN TO THE DEAN AGAIN!"

Harrison: (looking dazed) "HUH?"

panel 5: Rita and Harrison outside pub that resembles an old castle - the sign reads: WIZARD'S CASTLE

After classes

Rita: "COME ON, HARRISON, THE LEAST YOU CAN DO FOR ME AFTER I SAVED YOU IN CLASS IS TO BUY ME A BREW!"

Harrison: "YES - YES SURE, RITA ... THANKS."

panel 1: Rita and Harrison entering inside the pub - the pub
is filled with people, a waitress is serving - the
pub is decorated with swords displayed on walls.

Rita: (pointing) "THERE'S AN EMPTY TABLE IN THAT CORNER."

panel 2: A waitress is taking Rita and Harrison's order.

Rita: "WE'LL HAVE TWO TANKARDS OF ALE."

panel 3: Harrison holding tankard in hand.

Harrison: "IT'S NOT A DAYDREAM RITA ... IT'S SOMETHING INSIDE
ME ... SOMETHING I'VE GOT TO FINISH!"

panel 4: Rita and Harrison toasting - clicking tankards
together. We see behind them one of those swords
displayed on wall.

Rita: "WELL YOU'D BETTER FINISH IT ON YOUR OWN TIME OR THE
DEAN IS GOING TO THROW YOU OUT OF THIS SO-CALLED
SCHOOL OF HIGHER LEARNING. LET'S DRINK TO THAT!"

Harrison: "YES - YES SURE." (with a faraway look in his eyes)

panel 5: Close up of Harrison bringing tankard to his lips and
looking off to the side as if he sees something.

Harrison: (daydreaming) AS THE COLD ALE TRICKLED DOWN MY
THROAT ... I SAW FROM THE CORNER OF MY EYE THE THING
I MUST ELIMINATE ... IT WAS NOT A DAYDREAM ... IT
HAD FOLLOWED ME HERE!!

panel 1:   Harrison jumps up from his chair and is about to
           grab one of those decorative swords off the wall.

Harrison: "I'M NOT DAYDREAMING NOW ... I'M NOT!"

panel 2:   Harrison standing like a madman, swinging the sword
           through the air - patrons at pub are running in
           chaos.

Harrison: "I'LL SHOW YOU ALL THAT I'M NOT HAVING A DAYDREAM!"

panel 3:   A collage of 4 separate scenes of Harrison battling
           the monster. As each scene progresses, Harrison is
           winning.

Harrison: (in 4th scene) "DIE DIE DIE!"

page 5

panel 1:   Close up of Harrison's face - his eyes are glazed over.

Harrison: "I TOLD YOU RITA - THAT IT WAS SOMETHING I HAD TO DO ... IT WASN'T A DAYDREAM!"

panel 2:   Two policemen are leading Harrison out of pub; he is in a straightjacket. Off to the right is Rita in shock, with her hands to her face.

Harrison: "DIDN'T I TELL YOU THAT, RITA?"

panel 3:   Outside of pub Rita and a male are standing to the left as two other policemen carry off Harrison's victim on a stretcher.

Rita: (looking down) "HOW HORRIBLE! I CAN'T BELIEVE IT REALLY HAPPENED!"

Male: "WHATEVER DRUG HE WAS ON TURNED HIS HATRED INTO AN HALLUCINATION!"

panel 4:   Two policemen and a crowd of students standing near lamp post.

Cop #1:   "THIS KID'S TRIP TURNED REAL!"

Cop #2:   "I'LL SAY IT DID! I HAD MY PROBLEMS IN SCHOOL WITH THE DEAN BUT THEY GOT STRAIGHTENED OUT ..."

panel 5:   Same two policemen, cop #1 is holding the bloody sword that Harrison used.

Cop #2:   "I NEVER HEARD OF ANYONE HATING THIS MUCH!"

Cop #1:   "HE MUST HAVE HATED HIM A THOUSAND TIMES ... ONE FOR EACH PIECE HE CUT OFF ... WITH THIS!!"

END

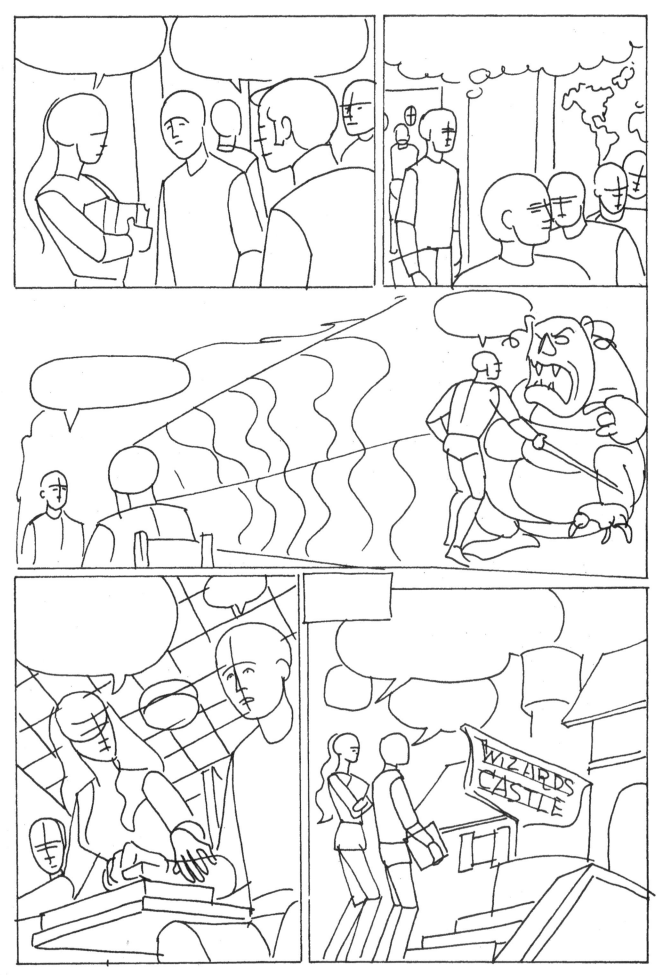

THERE'S AN EMPTY TABLE IN THAT CORNER.

WE'LL HAVE TWO TANKARDS OF ALE.

IT'S NOT A DAYDREAM, RITA .....IT'S SOMETHING INSIDE ME.....SOMETHING I'VE GOT TO FINISH!

WELL, YOU'D BETTER FINISH IT ON YOUR OWN TIME OR THE DEAN IS GOING TO THROW YOU OUT OF THIS SO-CALLED SCHOOL OF HIGHER LEARNING.

LET'S DRINK TO THAT!

YES-YES, SURE.

AS THE COLD ALE TRICKLED DOWN MY THROAT...I SAW FROM THE CORNER OF MY EYE THE THING I MUST ELIMINATE ....IT WAS NOT A DAYDREAM....IT HAD FOLLOWED ME HERE!!

Up to this point, we have been drawing very realistic
monsters. Now it's time to loosen up and draw

CARTOON MONSTERS

STEP 1.

In doing these cartoon monsters, you
will use much of what you've learned
in drawing realistic monsters.

STEP 2.

STEP 1.

STEP 2.

Keep the basic
shapes simple.

A good cartoon monster drawing deserves a good monster gag caption.

STEP 1.

Make the shapes
large and simple.

STEP 2.

STEP 1.

STEP 2.

Wrap the
bandages
around
the form.

STEP 1.

STEP 2.

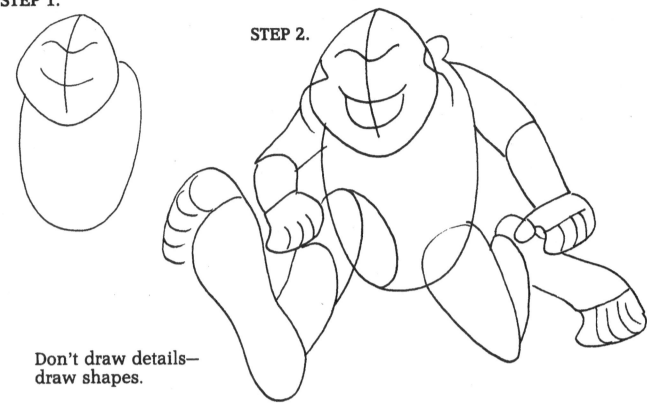

Don't draw details—
draw shapes.

STEP 1.

STEP 2.

Just as in drawing a
realistic monster, add
the details only after you
are satisfied with the
action and basic shapes.

STEP 3.

BIGFOOT IS GOING TO ITS SCHOOL DANCE... THE FOOTBALL!

STEP 3.

WHEN FRANKENSTEIN'S MONSTER THOUGHT OF THE OPERATION THAT PUT HIM TOGETHER, IT HAD HIM IN STITCHES!

If you are going to be a monster maker ... then there are many things you must know about monsters.

Can you answer a few monster questions from the syndicated newspaper feature ...?

TRIVIA TREAT
by Elvira and Tony Tallarico

Practice Page

Practice Page

Practice Page

Practice Page